FLAT STANLEY'S
ADVENTURES IN CLASSROOM 2E

Siɨma kíntu

Don't miss any of Flat Stanley's Adventures in Classroom 2E!

Class Pet Surprise
Riding the Slides

Or his Worldwide Adventures!

The Mount Rushmore Calamity
The Great Egyptian Grave Robbery
The Japanese Ninja Surprise
The Intrepid Canadian Expedition
The Amazing Mexican Secret
The African Safari Discovery
The Flying Chinese Wonders
The Australian Boomerang Bonanza
The US Capital Commotion
Showdown at the Alamo
Framed in France
Escape to California
The Midnight Ride of Flat Revere
On a Mission for Her Majesty
Lost in New York

The 100th Day

Created by **Jeff Brown**
Written by **Kate Egan**
Pictures by **Nadja Sarell**

HARPER
An Imprint of HarperCollinsPublishers

Contents

Class Party

It was the end of the day at Maple Shade Elementary School. Stanley Lambchop was in his classroom looking at a clock.

This was not the kind of clock he had at home with big numbers on an electronic screen.

This clock was round with two hands that moved in a circle. The little hand showed the hour, and the big hand showed the minute.

Stanley's teacher, Ms. Root, did not have to wait for time to move the hands on this clock. She could move them around all by herself! This was a special clock she used to teach her students about telling time.

Right now, Ms. Root was standing in the middle of the classroom, holding the clock so everyone could see.

She moved the little hand to the eight and the big hand to the twelve. "Can anyone tell me what time it is now?"

That was easy! Stanley put his hand up. So did his best friend, Marco, who was sitting next to him. Marco had been doodling in a notebook, but

he never missed a chance to answer a question.

"Yes, Stanley," she called, but Marco chimed in at the same time. "Eight o'clock," the boys said together.

"Correct!" said Ms. Root, excitedly. She was excited about *everything*! That was one reason why all the kids loved Ms. Root.

Next, she moved the hands so that the big hand was on the four. The little hand was between the eight and the nine.

"I know what that is!" one of Stanley's classmates shouted, jumping out of her chair.

"Hang on," Ms. Root told the whole

class. "This time, I have a challenge question."

Ms. Root pointed to the clock's hands. "Look at this time," she said. "Now . . . can anyone tell me how many minutes have passed *since* it was eight o'clock?"

That was a challenge, for sure! Stanley Lambchop did not know the answer.

Stanley leaned toward Marco and whispered, "How many minutes are between the twelve and the four?"

"Well, it's five minutes between each number, right?" Marco whispered back. "So it's five plus five plus five plus five."

Wait a minute . . . Stanley thought.

Ms. Root was up to something sneaky!

The teacher called on their class-mate Sophia. "Twenty minutes have passed since eight," Sophia announced. "And now it is eight twenty."

"Very nice!" said Ms. Root.

She noticed that Stanley had his hand in the air again. "Would you like to add something, Stanley?"

He said, "I don't think that was a question about time, Ms. Root. I think that was a question about *math*!"

Ms. Root put the clock down and smiled. "You caught me, Stanley," she admitted. "I like to do math whenever we can. It is an important part of telling time, after all." It was just like Ms. Root to do that, Stanley thought. You never knew when she was going to sneak math into some other part of the day. She could slip math into science or reading as easily as Stanley could slip into a narrow space. And that was pretty easily!

Stanley could fit in small spaces because he was flat. One day, not that long ago, a bulletin board had fallen off his bedroom wall and landed right on top of him. Stanley was not hurt, but now he was as flat as a piece of paper.

Stanley's flatness let him do things that other kids couldn't do, like slide under a door or fold himself small enough to fit in an envelope. He could even trick people with his flatness . . . just like Ms. Root was tricking the class!

"Speaking of *time* . . ." she continued. "There is something important we need to discuss. Pretty soon it will be *time* for our class to have a celebration!"

"That's right," joked Marco. "My birthday is just around the corner!"

The kids cracked up. Everyone knew that Marco's birthday was last week!

When the laughter died down, Ms. Root spoke again. "Friends, this Friday will be the Hundredth Day of School!"

Stanley remembered the Hundredth Day of School from when he

100th Day of School Party

was in first grade. Now that he was in second grade, it seemed like a long time ago.

"Last year, everyone had to bring something from home on that day," said Stanley's classmate Evan. "Well, not one something. *One hundred somethings!*"

"I brought in a hundred LEGOs," Elena remembered.

"I brought in a hundred bouncy balls," said Stevie.

"Then you dropped the box they were in," Marco pointed out. "And they bounced all over the floor, remember?"

Stanley remembered something else. "We helped Stevie pick up the bouncy balls. And then we did some math with them!" he told Ms. Root. "You would have loved it! We put them into groups of two and five and ten and twenty—"

"So are we doing it all again this year?" Sophia broke in. She seemed super excited. "I have a sticker collection now. I can bring a hundred stickers!"

"Well, friends, I have a different idea," Ms. Root said. "I was wondering what you all would think about having a class party."

"A party?" Marco cheered. "Yes!" He turned to give Stanley a high five.

This was another reason everyone loved Ms. Root. She liked to make sure her students had a good time!

Stanley knew what Ms. Root was up to, though.

"Not just any party, right?" he said. "It sounds like this will be a *math* party."

Ms. Root shook her head. "The Hundredth Day of School is different for different grades. This year, we will not work quite as much with numbers. We will just celebrate a hundred days together as a classroom family!"

Really? thought Stanley. It wasn't like Ms. Root to miss a chance to teach something to her class. But it was all right with him, he decided. While Stanley Lambchop liked math, he liked a celebration even better. And this one sounded like a ton of fun!

His classmate Josie raised her hand. Josie liked to make sure people were following the rules. "A party during school?" she asked. "How will that work?"

"Well," Ms. Root said, "I thought that should be up to the class!"

The class was quiet for a minute. Only Ms. Root would leave the party planning up to second graders!

Juniper raised her hand first. "I think we should have a sign-up sheet," she said. "Everyone can sign up to bring something in."

"Like decorations!" Sophie called out.

"And games . . ." Evan added.

"And food!" said Elena. "We can't forget the food!"

Stevie was shaking his head. He was worried about something. Stevie worried about a lot of things. "That is all the fun stuff," he said. "But we also need things like plates and napkins, right?"

"Thank you, Stevie!" said Ms. Root. "We will need to plan every detail to make sure our party is a success."

Stanley could hear people in the hallway now. Mr. Johnson's second graders, from the classroom next door, had been dismissed for the day. From the classroom window, Stanley could see a line of yellow school buses arriving to take everybody home.

"We will do more planning tomorrow, friends," said Ms. Root. "Tonight's homework is this: Please think about what you would like to share with the class at our party!"

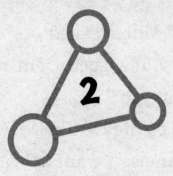

Pancakes

Just a few minutes later, Stanley and Marco were on the school bus, riding home. They always sat together in the same seat, behind Stanley's younger brother, Arthur.

Arthur was looking out the window. Stanley and Marco were talking about the party coming up in Classroom 2E.

"So what are you going to bring,

Stanley?" Marco asked.

Stanley shrugged. "I'm not sure. How about you?"

Marco pointed to himself with both of his thumbs. "I want to bring something that only Marco can bring," he said. "Or something that no one else will think of. Definitely not the napkins!"

That made sense to Stanley. Since Marco was the funniest kid in the class, he would need to bring something that made people laugh.

"Evan mentioned games, right?" said Stanley. "How about some jokes?"

"I like it!" said Marco. "Like a hundred knock-knock jokes. Or a hundred riddles . . ."

Stanley shook his head. "Remember, it doesn't have to be a hundred," he said.

"Oh yeah," said Marco. "A math party without any math. Talk about funny!"

Just then the school bus hit a big bump. Stanley's backpack slid toward the front of the bus. Marco held on to the back of Arthur's seat to steady himself. But Stanley flew up into the air! Seat belts didn't always work for Stanley. The bump made him slip right over the strap!

A gust of wind from an open window kept Stanley airborne for a minute. He waved around up there like a flag! Then, before he knew it,

the breeze died down and he was lying on the floor.

Arthur turned around to look. "Are you okay?" he asked his brother.

Marco undid his seat belt and stood up. "Need a hand, Stanley?" he said.

Stanley grabbed Marco's hand, got to his feet, and brushed himself off.

"I'm fine," he said to Arthur. "Thanks!" he said to his best friend.

Stanley made himself smile, but his face was turning red.

Some older kids were staring at him. Marco, who was usually cheerful, seemed concerned. Even the bus driver was watching. Stanley met her eyes in the rearview mirror.

"I'm fine," he repeated. "Don't worry!" He wanted to pretend this had never happened. Nobody wanted to stand out on the school bus!

Now that he was back in his seat, Stanley acted like flying in the bus was no big deal. Luckily, Marco acted that way, too! He knew just what a friend should do.

"So maybe you should bring food to the party," Stanley said, getting back to their conversation. "A funny food, you know?"

"Yes!" said Marco. "Like . . . pickles maybe. Or pea soup!"

Stanley laughed, even louder than usual. No one would ever guess he was still embarrassed.

"How about marshmallows?" he suggested.

Stanley thought marshmallows were the funniest food of all time. They looked big, but you could squish them down till they were almost nothing. Even their name was funny.

"Sweet!" said Marco. "Get it? That's perfect!"

Then the bus pulled up to his stop, and Marco put his backpack on in a hurry.

"See you tomorrow!" he called as he climbed out of the bus. Marco waved at Stanley as he walked away with his older sister.

Stanley's stop was next. Mr. Lambchop was waiting for him and

Arthur with a lot of questions. "How was your day, boys?" he asked. "Are you ready for a snack? What do you have for homework?"

Mr. Lambchop worked from home two days a week. When he came to the bus stop, he liked to know everything that happened at school. Today Arthur had a lot to tell him while

they walked home.

"Soon it will be the Hundredth Day of School!" he said. "I need to bring a hundred somethings in to show my class."

"Just like I did last year!" Stanley reminded him.

"And I need to dress up in a costume," Arthur continued. "I need to look like I am one hundred years old!"

"I never got to do that!" said Stanley. "No fair!"

Mr. Lambchop could not wait to help out. "You'll need a gray wig, I'd say," he suggested.

"And a cane!" added Arthur.

Stanley knew that not all old people used canes. Their grandmother walked on her own two feet!

"But . . ." he broke in. His words were drowned out by his father and brother.

"Sounds like we'll need to find some old clothes," said Mr. Lambchop. "If we don't have any at home, we could try a secondhand store."

They were almost to their house now. No one was listening to Stanley!

"I know, I know!" said Arthur, excited about planning his costume. "How about a bow tie?"

"I think I might have one of those upstairs," said Mr. Lambchop. "From back in my college days . . ."

They arrived at their house, and Mr. Lambchop opened the door.

Stanley dropped his backpack in the kitchen and went right to his room. He could get a snack in a little while, when his family was ready to talk to him again. He would tell his father what happened on the bus, too.

Stanley lay down on his bed, with his hands under his head. He looked at the ceiling.

He was still thinking about the party in Classroom 2E. Marshmallows would be perfect for Marco. He would bring a funny food, because he was a funny kid. But what would be perfect for *Stanley* to bring to the party? What kind of kid was Stanley?

Well, Stanley was a lot of things.

He was a good brother and a good friend. He loved his class, and he loved playing basketball.

But he knew what most people saw first when they looked at him. Stanley Lambchop was a flat kid. Except for once in a while—like today—he *liked* being a flat kid.

So a flat kid should bring a flat food, of course! Now it was all clear to Stanley.

Stanley knew many party foods were flat. Pizza. Cookies. Some kinds of chips. But none of those felt special. Every party had pizza and cookies and chips. Stanley wanted to bring something different, like marshmallows.

He thought and thought. Suddenly he sat up. He had it!

They were sweet, like marshmallows.

They were flat, like Stanley.

You never saw them at a party, Stanley realized. But they were delicious!

Stanley tore open his door and ran to the kitchen. Mr. Lambchop and Arthur were sitting at the table, eating pretzels, and talking about his costume. Pretzels would be good for a twisty kid, but Stanley Lambchop knew what was right for *him*.

And when Stanley had a good idea, nothing could stop him.

"Dad!" he exclaimed, interrupting.

"My class is celebrating the Hundredth Day of School, too. We are having a party, and I want to bring something special. Do you think you could help me make some pancakes?"

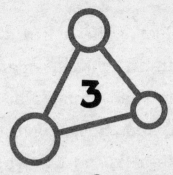

Party Planning

In school the next day, Ms. Root started the morning with announcements, just like she always did. There was a weather report so the kids would know if they needed to wear rain boots at recess. There was an announcement about today's school lunch, which would be grilled cheese sandwiches. Finally, after all of that was over, Juniper raised her hand.

"Ms. Root?" she asked. "Can we finish planning the class party?"

Juniper had made a sign-up sheet, but Ms. Root suggested that they make a list on the whiteboard instead. "That way we can all see what our friends will be sharing," said Ms. Root.

Stanley looked at Marco and shrugged. They shared a look that said "Good idea!"

Josie started things off. "I looked up some activities for the Hundredth Day of School," she said. "We can do them at our party!"

Back in first grade, they had played a lot of math games on the Hundredth Day of School, but Josie's

The Hundredth Day of School
PARTY

ideas were not really about counting. They were about moving around and having fun! "We can warm up with jumping jacks," she said.

"Sounds like gym class!" said Elena. Gym class was her favorite part of the week.

Josie grinned. "And that's not all!" she said. "After the jumping jacks, we will be ready for the main event. We will have a Hundredth Day Dance Party! One hundred seconds of dancing and then a rest. And then another hundred seconds of dancing! Over and over again with different music every time."

"I love it!" said Ms. Root. She danced in place for a minute to show she'd be part of the action, too. "I'll make the playlist!"

Evan had done some research of his own. "We can also build something in our classroom," he announced. The whole class could work together to make something out of one hundred cups! "All we need is some masking tape," he explained. "It's not about the number of cups, but about what we can do with them. It can be a classroom challenge!"

This day was sounding better and better to Stanley! He loved being in second grade. He loved doing something a little different for the Hundredth Day of School.

Juniper made a circle around the

activities on the board. "Looks like we're all set for fun!" she said. "Now can we talk about the decorations?"

Sophia raised her hand. She was really excited about the decorations. "I will bring some streamers!" she volunteered.

Evan had another idea for something. "I will make a chain of construction-paper loops," he said.

"I will bring balloons!" Stevie added.

"A hundred balloons?" Evan asked.

"That is too many balloons," said Juniper firmly. "We will need to save some space for the food!" She moved on to a new section of the board.

Everyone had ideas about the food.

"I'll bring cupcakes!" said Sophia.

"I'll bring some pretzels!" Juniper added.

"I'll bring my famous popcorn balls," said Ms. Root.

Elena waved her hand. "My mom always likes to bring fruit for parties," she said. "So you can sign me up for that."

"Thank you, Elena!" said Ms. Root. "It is always good to have a healthy option."

Marco's hand was up. He had been waiting a long time for Juniper to call on him, but now he just blurted out what he was bringing in. "I'll bring the marshmallows," he said.

Juniper paused before she wrote

that on the board. "Just plain marsh-mallows?" she said. She did not seem to like the idea.

Stanley Lambchop had to step in! "Can't have a party without marsh-mallows," he said, winking at his best friend. Marco grinned back.

"Okay . . ." Juniper said slowly. "Anyone else? Stanley, what are you bringing?"

"I'm bringing a stack of pancakes," he announced. "I can make two for each of us!"

The room went quiet for a moment.

Juniper looked at him strangely. "Pancakes aren't really party food, you know," she said.

Elena added, "Most people eat

them for breakfast."

Stanley knew that, of course! "But pancakes are my . . . my signature dish," he stammered. "Like Ms. Root's famous popcorn balls. No one can make flatter pancakes than Flat Stanley."

His classmates just looked confused. No one smiled or laughed. Not even Marco! Stanley's joke fell flat!

"I love your imagination, Stanley!" Ms. Root said brightly. "Pancakes will be the perfect addition to the party!"

The class moved on to wrap up some other details. Someone would bring the cups and napkins. Someone would bring the forks and knives. Stanley knew he would bring the maple syrup, but he did not raise his hand to say so. He was embarrassed again, like he had been on the bus. When his classmates didn't like his ideas, it felt like they didn't like *him*.

And no one was standing up for him. Not even his best friend!

The board was covered in ideas now. "I think that's all," said Juniper. She was ready to sit down when

The Hundredth Day of School
PARTY

Activities:
• Jumping jacks
• Dance party
• Build something

Decorations:
• Streamers
• Construction paper
• Balloons

Food
• Cupcakes
• Pretzels
• Popcorn balls
• Fruit
• Marshmallows
• Pancakes
• Cups and napkins
• Forks and knives

Sophia raised her hand.

"How many streamers should I bring?" Sophia asked. "Not a hundred, right? But how many?"

Juniper nodded. "Good question," she said. "Let's plan to bring one of everything for each kid in the class."

"There are fifteen of us . . ." said Josie.

"So that means fifteen streamers, fifteen balloons, fifteen cookies, and the rest," Evan finished. Juniper wrote all the numbers on the whiteboard.

And thirty pancakes, thought Stanley. So we can each have two. That would not take too long to make with his dad, he figured. And Marco would bring fifteen marshmallows, he thought automatically.

He turned to look at Marco, trying to catch his eye, but his friend was doodling in a notebook. He was not paying attention to Stanley at all.

Stanley tried to shake it off. He sat up extra straight in his chair. He listened closely as Ms. Root introduced something new.

"Now, friends," she said, "as you know, we are not the only class celebrating the Hundredth Day of School."

"The kids in my brother's class are dressing up like they are one hundred years old!" Stanley called out.

His classmates smiled. A couple

of people said, "Cool!" But Marco did not look up from what he was drawing. Stanley frowned.

"Our party will celebrate our classroom family," said Ms. Root. "But we will also be celebrating our whole second-grade family on the Hundredth Day of School. That is why we will be doing a special project with the other second-grade class. After lunch today, Mr. Johnson's class will be joining us for art!"

Stanley thought Marco might like that. He loved art, after all. For a moment, Marco looked excited—he even pumped his fist in the air.

While Ms. Root was speaking, though, Marco's eyes were back on his notebook. Was something wrong? Was there a reason Marco was ignoring him? Stanley did not know what it could be.

Ms. Root said, "We will need to put paper on the wall for our project. We will need to get some paints and brushes ready. Would anyone like to give me a hand during lunch?"

That would mean skipping lunch to eat in the classroom with Ms. Root. Most days, Stanley would not want to skip lunch. He would be having fun with Marco! Today he was not so sure about that.

So, before anyone else could beat him to it, Stanley raised his hand. "I can do it," he said. "I am happy to help."

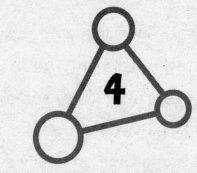

Rainbow Handprints

Stanley barely had a chance to eat his lunch—a salami sandwich, an apple, and a juice box—while he was helping Ms. Root. There was a lot to do before Mr. Johnson's class came into Classroom 2E!

Ms. Root did not tell him what the art project would be, but Stanley could see that it was something big. He helped Ms. Root stretch a huge piece of paper over the whiteboard. It covered up the lists that Juniper had made. It also covered up some bookshelves on the far side of the room! "Let's put some tape on every edge of the paper to make sure it stays up," Ms. Root said, and they did.

When they were done, Ms. Root asked, "Could you pour some paints into these bowls, Stanley?"

The bowls were low and wide, like soup bowls. Stanley poured yellow paint into one of them. He poured blue, red, purple, and green paint into some others.

Whatever they were doing would be in a rainbow of colors!

Stanley put paintbrushes next to

each bowl. He set up jars of water
for washing the paintbrushes. Then
Ms. Root said, "Oh, where will people
wash their hands?" Stanley was not
worried about that, but Ms. Root put
containers of wet wipes all over the
classroom.

Whatever they were doing, Ms.
Root expected it to be messy!

By the time the rest of the class came back from lunch, the room had been transformed. "What is going on?" Elena asked as she returned. "Are we even in the right place?" she joked.

"Friends, please make sure your desks are clear," said Ms. Root. "It's time to make space for art!"

When Classroom 2E was ready for guests, Ms. Root sent Stevie to knock on Mr. Johnson's door. In no time, the other second-grade class was walking into Ms. Root's room in a line.

Mr. Johnson had wild curly hair and a purple shirt. "Second graders!" he said in a loud voice. "Listen up!" When everyone was listening, he explained what the two classes would do.

Each student would have a partner from the other class, he said. One partner would cover the other partner's hand with paint. Then the student with a painted hand would press it against the paper!

"We're looking for a hundred handprints," Ms. Root explained.

"And we will hang this banner in the hallway for the Hundredth Day of School!" Mr. Johnson finished.

As soon as the teachers stopped talking, the students found their partners and got to work. Stanley usually picked Marco as a partner for everything. Today, though, Marco's partner was a boy in a baseball cap. Marco laughed with him in the way he usually laughed with Stanley.

Stanley's partner was a girl named Sam. She had sparkly earrings and a friendly smile. "Let's do my hand first," she suggested. She was not Marco, but she seemed nice.

"Sure!" Stanley shrugged. "That works," he said. He picked up a paintbrush and dipped it in yellow paint. Once he had a big glob of paint, he spread it all over Sam's hand!

Sam giggled. "It looks like my hand is covered in mustard!" she said.

That gave Stanley an idea. "I'll do mine in red, okay? Like ketchup!"

"Yes!" said Sam. She had to make

her handprint before she could paint Stanley's hand, though. Stanley led her through the crowded classroom, saying "Excuse me, excuse me . . ." so Sam did not bump into anyone by mistake.

"Coming through!" he announced. He walked right by Marco without saying a word.

Sam pressed her yellow hand onto the paper. There was so much paint on it that her handprint dripped! "Can I do another one?" she asked Mr. Johnson, who was standing nearby.

"Yes!" he said. "Remember, we are aiming for one hundred handprints!"

"So . . . how many handprints can I make?" Sam asked her teacher.

Stanley Lambchop could figure this out!

"How many kids are in your class?" Stanley asked Sam.

"Our class is really small," she said. "We have only ten kids!"

And Ms. Root's class has fifteen students. Fifteen kids plus ten kids from Mr. Johnson's room equaled twenty-five kids.

Stanley knew that a quarter was twenty-five cents, and he knew that four quarters equaled one dollar. So there were four sets of twenty-five in one hundred.

"That means each kid gets to make four handprints!" he told Sam. "We'd better get back to work!"

Sam slathered red paint all over Stanley's hand, and he made his ketchup handprint right next to Sam's mustard one. Then they washed their hands and started all over again.

"What colors should we do next?" he asked her.

"I'll do blue, and you do orange," she said. "Those are my two favorite colors."

Stanley liked those colors, too, because they were the colors of his favorite baseball team. But by the time he'd painted her palm blue and headed back to the hanging paper, there was a problem.

The large piece of paper he had helped tape up earlier was falling down!

Ms. Root and Mr. Johnson tried to fix it with more tape. But *that* was a problem, too. To add more tape, they had to stand in front of the paper, and now the paper was covered in paint!

"Uh-oh!" said Ms. Root. She got too close to the paper and got paint all over her sleeve.

Stanley Lambchop walked over to

the teachers. He knew he could help solve this problem.

"I have an idea!" he said to Ms. Root. "Can someone give me a lift?"

"A lift?" said Mr. Johnson.

"If you pick me up, I'll be able to reach the top of the paper without getting covered in paint," Stanley explained.

"Oh, I see!" said Mr. Johnson. He moved toward the board and made his hands into a platform for Stanley to step on. Then he lifted his hands until Stanley was as high as the top corner of the paper.

"Could you turn around a little, please?" Stanley asked politely.

Mr. Johnson turned so that

Stanley's back was against the wall. It looked like he was taped up right next to the paper!

Carefully, Stanley moved his hand toward the part of the paper that was falling down. Since he was flat, he did not have to be in front of the paper. He could reach it from above, and from the side, so he was safe from the paint!

"Let me get you some more tape," Ms. Root said. She gave him so many pieces of tape that they went through the whole roll. There was no way the paper would fall down now!

When Stanley was finished, Mr. Johnson lowered him to the ground. A few of Stanley's classmates clapped

for him—but not Marco, he noticed. Now Marco was drawing something on the corner of the big paper. What was going on with his best friend? Stanley wondered.

Luckily, Stanley had a new friend. Sam was waiting with a bowl of orange paint. She spread it all over Stanley's hand, and Stanley made another handprint! Stanley and Sam made four handprints each, all on the same part of the paper. "Our handprints are playing together!" Sam said.

"*We* can play together at recess!" Stanley said.

When her class lined up to leave, Sam called to Stanley from across the classroom. "I'll see you on the playground, right?" she asked.

The first and second graders all had recess at the same time. Stanley would definitely see Sam on the playground later! Which was lucky, he thought, because he would probably not be playing with Marco.

Too bad Sam wouldn't be at the class party.

Unless . . .

Suddenly Stanley Lambchop had another great idea.

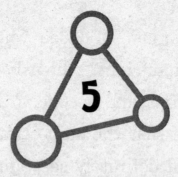

Special Guests

Ms. Root's class washed the paint-brushes and wiped their desks. It was time for music, then reading, then recess. Stanley's class was so busy that he did not get to share his great idea right away.

But he did get to play with Sam! She was waiting for him at afternoon recess and called him over to jump rope with two of her friends.

"This is Stan," Sam told her friends. "These are Kayla and Izzy," she told Stanley. Kayla was in a red coat, and Izzy was wearing a bright striped scarf.

Kayla and Izzy were each turning one end of a long rope. As soon as they lifted it off the ground, Sam rushed underneath and started jumping. While the girls turned, Sam sang a little song.

"Bubble gum, bubble gum, in a dish. How many pieces do you wish?" Sam chanted.

"One . . . two . . . three . . ." Kayla and Izzy counted.

For some reason, the counting made Stanley think of Ms. Root. She would love hearing numbers on the playground!

Kayla and Izzy got all the way up to sixteen. Then Sam missed the rope, and her turn was over.

"Want to try it, Stan?" said Izzy.

People did not usually call Stanley Lambchop "Stan," but he didn't mind it.

And Stanley Lambchop did not usually jump rope at recess.

But it was good to try new things, Stanley thought. "Uh, sure," he said. It was like having pancakes at a party!

It turned out that jumping rope was not that hard. Stanley just had to make sure the breeze on the

playground did not knock him off balance. Soon he found a rhythm, and the girls counted each jump. He got all the way up to twenty-three!

While he jumped, he could see what other kids were doing on the playground. It looked like there was a big game of tag going on with the first graders and second graders all together. Marco was chasing Stanley's brother, Arthur! At least he was playing with one of the Lambchops, Stanley thought.

When recess was over, Stanley said goodbye to Sam and lined up to go back to Ms. Root's room. The kids had a bathroom break and a water break before they were finally back at their desks. The minute the class-room was quiet, Stanley raised his hand.

"Do you have a question about spelling, Stanley?" Ms. Root asked. This was the time of day when they usually practiced their spelling words.

"I don't have a question at all," Stanley admitted. "I have an excellent *idea!*"

After waiting for such a long time, he talked very fast. "What if we invite some special guests to our party on Friday? I was thinking we could include Mr. Johnson's class," he said.

To Stanley's surprise, Marco chimed in, too. "Almost double the guests? That will make the party twice as fun!"

He looked over at Stanley and grinned. Stanley wasn't sure what to do.

Stevie frowned. "If we have almost double the guests, then we will need almost double of everything else," he pointed out.

"That's what I was thinking," said Sophia. "Double the streamers . . ."

"And double the cups for the building challenge," said Evan.

Double the pancakes, too! Stanley thought.

Ms. Root did not seem concerned about that. "Well, I think you can all figure that out together," she said.

"I know how many kids are in Mr. Johnson's class," Stanley said. He had asked Sam earlier when they were making handprints.

"Thank you, Stanley. That is some important information," said Ms. Root.

"There are ten of them . . ." Stanley began.

"And fifteen of us," Marco said. He finished Stanley's sentence, just like old times. Stanley smiled back at him, but he was still unsure.

"Twenty-five students altogether," said Ms. Root. "So what do we think, friends? Should we invite Mr. Johnson's class to celebrate with us? Let's have a show of hands."

Everyone's hand went up!

Juniper's list was still on the board. Ms. Root went back to it and erased all the fifteens. Then she put a 25 in front of all the items. Twenty-five cups and napkins, twenty-five pretzels, twenty-five popcorn balls and marshmallows. And fifty pancakes, two for each of us.

"We can do this!" Ms. Root said. She clapped excitedly. "It's a plan!"

But that was not the end of the discussion. Now Marco's hand was up, and he had an idea of his own. An idea that was inspired by Stanley!

"Marco?" said Ms. Root. "Do you have something to add?"

Stanley was not sure, but he

thought Marco winked at him before he spoke.

Marco said, "We all loved Stanley's idea, right? But I say why stop there?"

Marco stood up and walked around the room, raising his voice like he was giving a big speech. "I say we invite the whole first grade, too! We can have the party right after recess, when the kids in both grades are all together anyway. How about a show of hands?"

Ms. Root shook her head and smiled. Sometimes she did not know what to do with Marco.

But everyone loved the idea! They all raised their hands.

"Yes!" said Elena. "There is one rule for good parties: the bigger the better!"

"And remember, the first graders will all be wearing costumes," Stanley said. He could not wait to see his brother, Arthur, in his gray wig.

Only Josie was concerned. "Hold on," she said. "How many people is that?"

The kids looked around at each other, but no one knew the number of first graders in their school. Finally, Ms. Root jumped in. "I think I can find that out," she said.

She opened her laptop and clicked through some screens. It did not take long for her to get the facts. "Okay, friends. There are two first-grade classes," she said. "One with twelve students, and one with thirteen."

Josie did some addition in her head. "Twelve plus thirteen is twenty-five. That means there's the same number of first graders and second graders," she said.

"We'll be even!" said Evan.

"And twenty-five plus twenty-five is fifty guests!" said Marco. "Which is half of one hundred, by the way. Which is perfect for the Hundredth Day of School!"

Stevie shook his head and raised his hand. "We do not have space for fifty people," he said. "Where will everyone sit?"

"That is a good point," said Ms. Root. For a moment, even the teacher was stumped.

But Elena thought of something. "I don't think we need to change the party," she said. "We just need to change the location. Do you think we could set up our things in the gym?"

"Yes!" Marco high-fived Elena. "That's it!" he said.

Ms. Root nodded. "Yes, yes," she agreed. "That's a great idea. I will speak to the principal. If we move this party to the gym, it will work!"

They had not invited the other classes yet, but Stanley was sure they would say yes. Who could resist a party?

"The gym will be a great place for our dance party," Sophia pointed out.

"Plus our building project," said Juniper.

"But that's not all," Stevie pointed out. He was still worried. "We need to double everything all over again. Twenty-five plus twenty-five, right? We'll need extra food and decorations. Not to mention tables and chairs!"

Stanley turned around in his seat to look at Stevie. "Do we need to have tables?" he asked. "Can't people just walk around with their snacks?"

That's what he had seen at grown-up parties. He had seen it at birthday parties, too.

"No one needs a table and chairs

for marshmallows or popcorn balls," Juniper said, agreeing with Stanley. "Those are finger foods!"

Marco agreed with Stevie, though. "I don't know. It could get messy."

Stanley's feelings were hurt again . . . until he heard what Marco had to say.

"Don't forget the most important party food. No one can eat it standing up!"

"The pretzels? The fruit?" the kids in the class guessed.

"No!" said Marco. "You're forgetting what's going to make this a party to remember!" This time Marco definitely winked at Stanley. "The pancakes!"

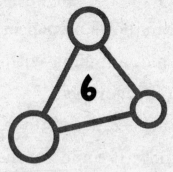

Math Surprise

When Stanley and Marco settled into their usual seats on the bus, Marco acted like nothing had happened at school. Stanley was confused. He was glad to have his best friend back. But he wanted to know why Marco had stopped speaking to him.

Then Marco told him. Or . . . he told him something else, which explained it all.

"I've got something for you, Stan," said Marco. He grinned. "If I can call you that," he added.

Stanley laughed. "That's what Sam's friends called me," he said. "But I think I'll stick with Stanley!"

Marco held out a piece of paper, and Stanley took it. He looked at it in wonder.

Stanley Lambchop had a hard time drawing things that he could see in his head.

Marco Ramirez, though, could draw *anything*.

This was a drawing of a superhero in action. And it was not just any superhero. This was a made-up super-hero named Flat Super-Stanley!

"I'm sorry I stayed away from you today," Marco said. "But I started making this awesome sketch for you, and I didn't want to give away the secret till it was done. You know I can't keep a secret."

Stanley laughed. Keeping secrets

was hard for Marco because he loved to talk.

Stanley looked at it and smiled. Flat Super-Stanley was flat, just like the real Stanley. He had a cape and a mask, plus something rolled up in his hand. Was it a garden hose?

"I love it!" said Stanley.

Marco said "Flatness is your superpower, right? So it really bothered me that no one liked your idea to bring flat pancakes to the party. Sure, most parties don't have pancakes. But that's why pancakes rock! Anyway, this picture shows how super you really are."

He laughed and pointed at the

rolled-up thing. "That did not turn out so great," Marco said. "But it's your secret weapon. See? It's a jump rope! You never know when you might need it."

Stanley's smile was as wide as a basketball hoop. "Of course!" he said. "I see it now! This is awesome, Marco!" he said.

"I did not want you to get mixed up. People might not like your idea for the party. But they still like *you*. And I bet they will like the pancakes, too," Marco said.

"And after Friday, maybe *every* party will have pancakes," Stanley joked. "Plus marshmallows."

"Or marshmallow pancakes!"

Marco suggested. "Don't tell anyone, but I also drew a little Flat Super-Stanley in the corner of the banner we made. Just for fun! I might draw him in some other places, too."

The bus was slowing down, and Marco's eyes got wide. "Oh! It's my stop!" he said. He scrambled for his backpack, rushed into the aisle, and called back over his shoulder to Stanley. "Glad you like my picture! See you tomorrow, superfriend!"

Stanley was lucky to have a friend like Marco in Classroom 2E, he thought. He could not wait to celebrate one hundred days with their class!

* * *

That afternoon, Stanley made a chart at home. His chart listed every hour between today at dinnertime and Friday at party time. Too bad the party was not tomorrow. It was the day *after* tomorrow! That felt like a long way off. But maybe the chart would make the time pass by a little faster! When Stanley counted up all the hours, he saw that there were forty-four left to go. He would cross them off the chart one by one as the hours passed by.

When he woke up on Thursday, Stanley crossed off nine hours in a row. He had spent a lot of time asleep!

He kept the chart in his desk all

day at school and crossed off hours
when he could. Sometimes he was
busy doing other things, though. At
the end of the day, he was busy getting ready for the party!

Ms. Root's class gathered in the
school gym when all the gym classes
were over. They would set some

things up today so they would be ready tomorrow afternoon. The food and some of the decorations would arrive at the last minute.

Stanley quickly looked at his chart. There were only twenty-four hours till the party now!

Ms. Root rolled a cart to the center of the gym. Many chairs were on the cart, folded up and lying sideways. Some grown-up volunteers helped the kids take the chairs off the cart and unfold them. Some other volunteers carried tables out of a closet and set them up around the gym. When the chairs were ready, kids carried them to the tables.

"We have fifty guests altogether,"

said Ms. Root. "So how many tables do we need?" She wanted her students to be mostly in charge of the party.

No one said anything until Josie piped up.

"I think that depends on how many kids are at each table. So . . . let's see how many chairs fit around each one," she suggested.

"Great thinking!" Ms. Root replied.

The gym grew loud with the sound of chairs scraping on the shiny floor. Stanley and Marco dragged fifteen chairs to one table and squeezed them all around. The chairs were so close to each other that they were all touching.

Stanley looked at the table. "This does not seem right to me, Marco," he said. "These chairs are packed very tight. Even Flat Super-Stanley would not be able to slip in or sit down!"

Marco grinned. "Unless he flew in from the top . . ." he pointed out. "Like you did when you fixed the banner."

But Marco pulled some chairs away. That made the table a lot less crowded.

"Okay, how many chairs do we have now?" Stanley asked.

"Ten altogether," Marco said, counting. "Four on each side and one on each end."

Stanley looked at them and nodded. "That seems better," he said.

Elena shouted from the other side of the gym. "Looks like ten chairs per table works best!" Her voice echoed against the wall.

Juniper took it from there, counting by tens. "So ten people at one table means twenty people at two tables, which means thirty people at three tables . . ." She got all the way to "fifty kids means we need five tables."

Ms. Root just smiled, like she knew something her students did not know. Stanley wondered what her secret was.

The kids placed five tables around the gym with ten chairs each. They set them up with plates and cups and napkins. Then they gathered at the

gym door to look at what they had done.

"We'll add the balloons tomorrow!" Stevie said. "Then it will be a real party!"

Sophia stared at the tables. She squinted. Then she said, "The tables are so far apart! We will have to yell if we want to talk to each other." She raised her voice when she said "yell," and Stanley heard another echo.

Marco had an idea. "Well, let's just move the tables closer to each other!"

"No!" Elena said. "I have a better idea. Let's put them in a circle."

Josie shook her head. "But rectangular tables can't *make* a circle!"

The class was stumped until

Stanley spoke up. After all, he knew a thing or two about things with flat sides.

"We could put them in a square," he said. "All we need is some extra tables."

Once again, Ms. Root gave a mysterious smile . . .

And suddenly Stanley knew what was up.

Pancake Math

While his classmates moved chairs and tables around the gym. Stanley walked up to his teacher. "Ms. Root," he said, "you are very tricky! But I can see what you are doing. You said this was not a math party, but we need math to do all the planning!"

"Is that so?" said Ms. Root. "Tell me what you mean." She was acting like she did not know. Stanley did not believe her!

Marco was there at his side. "Stanley is right!" he said. "There's math all over this party! It started with planning what we would bring. We needed math to know how much."

"And then we needed math for the handprints," Stanley added. "To make sure everyone got to make the same number of prints on the banner."

Some other kids joined the conversation. "I can't believe this!" Sophia said. "We have been doing math without even knowing it!"

"Like when we added guests to our party," said Elena. "That was actually . . . addition!"

"We added extra food and decorations, too," Evan chimed in.

Stanley took his chart out of his pocket. "I even made a chart and used math to count the hours until the party started," he explained. "As I crossed each hour off, the number of hours kept getting smaller. That was subtraction!"

"Don't forget what we are doing right now with the tables and chairs," Josie said. "Talking about the shapes for the tables—that's math. Figuring out the number of chairs for each table—that's math, too!"

"It's everywhere!" Stanley said, shaking his head.

Ms. Root threw her hands in the

air. "I give up!" she told the class. "You caught me!"

But no one minded if Ms. Root had been a little sneaky. She taught math the way she taught everything. By making it fun!

The next math problem was a little harder than any the class had done so far. When they made the tables into a square, they needed a lot more tables. Ms. Root helped the class think it through.

"If we put the table into a square," she said, "we only want people sitting on one side of the table."

Josie saw just what she meant. "That's right! The chairs can only be on the side that is facing into the square. If there were kids on the other side of the table, they would have their backs to the kids on the other side of the square."

The class already knew that each table could fit four kids on each side. They already knew there would be fifty kids altogether. So how many tables would they need?

It took a lot of counting for the class to find the answer. "Twelve tables!" Juniper yelled across the gym. "To fit forty-eight kids!"

"What?" said Stevie. "But that's not enough!"

But Josie was drawing a map on a napkin. "If we could make a square with three tables on each side, and four kids at each table, there would be two kids left over. But they could sit in chairs at the corner of the square. Problem solved!"

"We don't even need a building challenge after this," Evan said. "We have all worked together to build a party plan!"

The school day was almost over now. The class reset the plates, cups,

and napkins on the tables. And then it was time to say goodbye. Tomorrow would be the hundredth day of school!

Stanley crossed off one more hour on his chart. Twenty-three hours left until the party! He still had one big job left to do.

When Stanley and his brother got off the bus after school, Mrs. Lambchop was waiting for them. "Hi, boys. Dad had to work at the office today. But I'm ready to make some pancakes! Are you?" she asked.

"We're ready!" Stanley and Arthur said at the same time. They both loved helping out in the kitchen.

Especially when they were making something delicious!

The Lambchops usually made pancakes in the mornings. They usually ate them the minute they came out of the pan! But this was a special occasion.

Stanley and Arthur would make pancakes in the afternoon, before dinner. Stanley would bring them to school the next morning. And Ms. Root would heat them up right before the party.

Stanley and Arthur put on some chef's hats their grandmother had given them as gifts. Then, as Mrs. Lambchop read the recipe out loud, they started measuring. Each boy was working with his own bowl, because they needed to make so many pancakes! There would be at least two pancakes for each student at the party (even if some people decided not to eat them). And with fifty students, that meant one hundred pancakes!

"First we need two cups of flour," Mrs. Lambchop read from her cookbook. Stanley and Arthur measured the flour and put it in their bowls. There was a cloud of flour all around them!

They mixed in some baking powder, sugar, and salt. The next step was adding eggs and milk. But before Mrs. Lambchop could read out the rest of the recipe, there was a knock

at the Lambchops' front door.

"Hold on just a minute," Mrs. Lambchop told the boys. "I have been waiting for this package all day." She left the kitchen and walked through the house to the door. She took the cookbook with her by mistake.

Arthur looked at Stanley. "It's one egg and one cup of milk, remember?" he said. "We don't need to wait for the recipe. I remember it from the last time we made pancakes."

Arthur picked up an egg and cracked it into his bowl. Then he measured a cup of milk and poured it in. Stanley was helping Arthur mix it all together when Mrs. Lambchop returned.

She put the cookbook on the counter and said, "Excuse me one more minute, boys." Mrs. Lambchop took her package out to the garage.

Stanley finished helping Arthur, then went back to his own bowl. By then he couldn't remember the recipe anymore! Luckily the cookbook was right there. "Two eggs, two cups of milk," Stanley read. He put them in his bowl and mixed.

Stanley did not realize that he and Arthur had made different kinds of pancake batter by mistake!

Stanley's batter was perfect. When Mrs. Lambchop helped him ladle it onto a hot skillet, the pancakes grew fluffy and full of bubbles, just like they were supposed to. He flipped them and cooked the other side. By the time Stanley got through his bowl of batter, he had a stack of fifty pancakes.

But Arthur's batter did not seem to work. His first pancake was burned. His next pancake was flat and dry, almost like a cookie.

"This is strange," said Mrs. Lambchop. "It seems like something is wrong." She checked the temperature on the stove. She checked that there was enough butter in the pan. Finally, she said, "Arthur, did you follow the recipe?"

Arthur nodded. "Yep," he said. "I remembered it from last weekend."

"Wait. I'm not sure that you remembered it right. Didn't you only put in one cup of milk and one egg?"

"Oh! I'm sorry," Arthur said. "Do we need to start all over?"

"Not to worry," said Mrs. Lambchop briskly. "I think I can fix this problem." She cracked another egg. She measured out some milk. She added both things to Arthur's batter and put a scoop of the batter in the pan. This time, the pancake turned out just like Stanley's pancakes!

"Problem solved," said Mrs. Lambchop, smiling.

A problem, Stanley thought. Like a math problem.

And then he saw it! Just like party

planning, cooking was full of math. You had to add ingredients (or subtract them, if you were Arthur). You had to measure things with numbers. You had to make sure the numbers were correct. You could even tell if you had the wrong answer. If your math was wrong, your food would not taste right!

Stanley smiled. There was one more kind of math he would do at the party. He would add up the pancakes as he piled them on his plate!

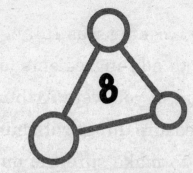

The Hundredth Day
of School

Stanley kept looking at his chart on the Hundredth Day of School. He was still counting the hours left until the party. The hours that seemed the longest were right before two o'clock! That was when everything would finally get started.

During math, the kids practiced adding numbers that equaled one

hundred. During spelling, they practiced big math words, like one million
and one billion. But the main event
was the party, and Ms. Root's students had to wait.

Stanley watched the classroom
clock. This clock was the round kind
with hands. He was glad Ms. Root
had taught them all how to tell time
on this clock. Too bad the minute
hand was so slow!

By the end of the school day, Stanley and Marco could hardly sit still. Stanley kept slipping out of his chair. Marco kept telling jokes during spelling. Finally, Ms. Root wiped the spelling words off the board. "Friends," she said, "it's time to join Mr. Johnson's class and the whole first grade in the gym!"

They lined up and walked quietly through the hallway. Then Ms. Root flung open the gym door and a regular afternoon became something special.

There was music in the gym now, with songs from Ms. Root's playlist. There were bunches of balloons on the tables, and a special table that held

the hundredth-day treats. Stanley was not sure he could eat one hundred things, but he definitely wanted to eat one of every item on the table!

The first graders were the next to arrive. Some of them were walking with canes, like a person who was one hundred years old. Some of them were wearing bathrobes. One girl had pink curlers in her hair!

Arthur waved at Stanley and Marco from across the gym. He was wearing plaid pants and a sweater vest. The hair in his gray wig was neatly parted to one side. "Grandpa?" Marco called out to Arthur. "Is that you?"

When Mr. Johnson's class arrived

in the gym, Ms. Root welcomed everyone to the party. "In just one hundred days, we have built a wonderful family here at school," she said.

It was true, Stanley thought. On the first day of school, he had not known some of the kids in Ms. Root's class. Now they were all his friends! He was starting to make some friends in Mr. Johnson's class, too.

When Ms. Root stopped talking, it was time for the cup-building challenge. Back when Evan came up with the idea, it was just supposed to be one hundred cups for Ms. Root's class. Now there were several piles of cups, so everyone could get a chance to try. When Ms. Root said "Go!" different groups of kids would work together to build something cool. But they did not have a lot of time to do it!

Stanley and Marco were in a group with Sam and her friends. Some of the other groups built a tower and a fort. But Kayla and Izzy had an even better idea. Together, their group built a pyramid! When the time was up, the tower and the fort fell down right away. But the pyramid stood up straight and strong.

"Great job, Stan!" Sam said. "I knew we could do it!

Then it was time for the dance party. To get everyone warmed up, Elena led them all through one hundred jumping jacks!

"If this is just the warm-up, I don't know what the dancing will be like!" Stanley said to Arthur. "I'm already out of breath!"

The party was also a game, and the dancers got a little time to rest. Ms. Root blasted music for one hundred seconds at a time. During those one hundred seconds, everyone danced hard. But when the music stopped, the kids were supposed to stop, too! Anyone still dancing was out of the game.

Marco was one of the first kids out. "Once I get dancing," he told Stanley, "it's hard to stop!" Stanley was out on the next round, even though he stopped in time. His body was so flat that it just kept flapping, even after his feet stopped!

The last kids left were Arthur and Sam. Stanley did not know who to cheer for! It turned out that each one of them got a prize. One was for first graders, and one was for second graders. And no one minded about the prizes, anyway. Everyone was ready to eat!

Stanley put a pile of food on his plate. There was a popcorn ball and a couple of pretzels, there was some fruit and a cupcake. Stanley took two marshmallows because there were extras. And then he came to the pancakes!

The pancakes were piled in big

stacks on two plates. There were even two small bottles of syrup next to them, which Stanley brought from home. Stanley had been worried that no one would eat them. But there was a little crowd of kids around them. One of the first graders was pouring maple syrup all over her pancake. And she was making a mess! The syrup leaked off her plate. The bottle was dripping and getting sticky. Stanley looked around, but he could not find a grown-up to help.

The Hundredth Day was a celebration of numbers. While planning it, Stanley and his friends had discovered that math was everywhere. They had also done a lot of counting!

But there was another kind of counting, too, Stanley knew. The kind that came when people could count on you. That meant they could trust you would be a good friend. Stanley counted on Marco. And now his class was counting on him!

"Hang on a second," he said to the first grader with the syrup. "If you keep pouring the syrup like that, it will get all over the table. Plus there might not be enough for anyone else!"

Josie was standing behind him. "Once syrup gets on the table, it's hard to get off," she said. "I think we need some paper towels. Or maybe a tablecloth."

Ms. Root's class had not discussed

the cleanup. Stanley did not know where to find any paper towels. But he knew someone who could be a tablecloth if he needed to. It was Stanley Lambchop himself!

Josie moved the plates of pancakes, and Stanley spread himself out over the table. "It's just until we finish serving," he told the kids who

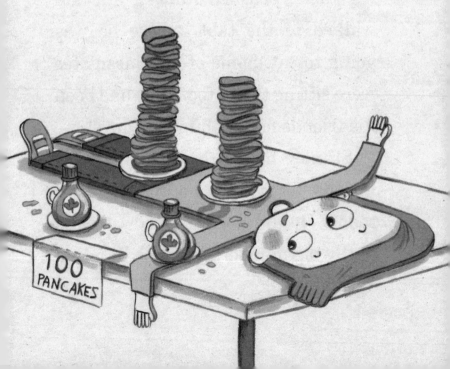

100 PANCAKES

gathered around him. "To save us from having a sticky mess!" Some syrup did get on his shirt. The plates on his belly tickled! But when all the pancakes were served, the table was as clean as it could be. Everyone had enough syrup. And Stanley's pancakes were still warm!

Stanley hopped off the serving table, brushed himself off, and walked to the table where he was going to eat. Some of his classmates were sitting there, too. They had been his friends for one hundred days!

Stanley hoped they would be his friends for many more days after today. He did not know how to add really big numbers over one hundred yet. But it would be one hundred plus one hundred plus one hundred plus one hundred . . . until infinity. Or at least until they finished second grade!

Stanley's 100th Day of School Pancake Recipe

To make Stanley's pancakes, you will only need a few things.

- 2 cups flour
- 2 teaspoons baking powder
- ¼ teaspoon salt
- 1 tablespoon sugar
- 2 eggs
- 1½ cups milk
- 2 tablespoons melted butter, cooled AND
- 1 grown-up to help with the stove!

Steps:

1. Heat a griddle or large skillet over medium-low heat.

2. In a bowl, mix the flour, baking powder, salt, and sugar together.

3. In another bowl, beat the eggs and milk together, then stir in the melted butter.

4. Gently stir this mixture into the dry ingredients, mixing only until you can't see the flour anymore.

5. Now you have some pancake batter, and it's okay if there are a few lumps.

6. Next, melt some extra butter on your skillet.

7. Then spoon some batter onto the skillet, making pancakes of any size you like!

8. Flip your pancake over once you see some bubbles in the batter and the bottom of the pancake looks light brown.

9. After flipping, cook until the second side is also light brown.

10. If you are making many pancakes, you can stack them up on a plate in a warm oven until you are ready to eat them!

Many people like syrup with their pancakes! But you can also eat them with peanut butter or cream cheese or jam or chocolate sauce . . . actually, you can eat pancakes with anything.

You can also add blueberries or chocolate chips in step seven. Delicious!